Many thanks to the friends and family
who helped me with this book.

CONTENTS

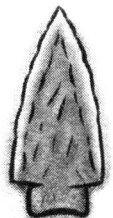

PREFACE

———

Grandpa and Grandma owned and operated Dillard's for forty-five years beginning in 1950. Locals would buy grocery goods and pick up mail from the country store, but it sat at the heart of their small community because of the warm conversation and genuine friendship so many of the visitors found there as well.

This series of short stories was written for my children as a way to pass on a piece of the country store. While they are not factual, many of the details contained within these pages are true. Little Frank was also found in my imagination, and could well have been any of Grandpa and Grandma's twenty grandchildren.

These stories are lighthearted and simple in nature, but I hope they convey my gratitude to have known Grandpa and Grandma and to have grown up visiting their country store.

The Author

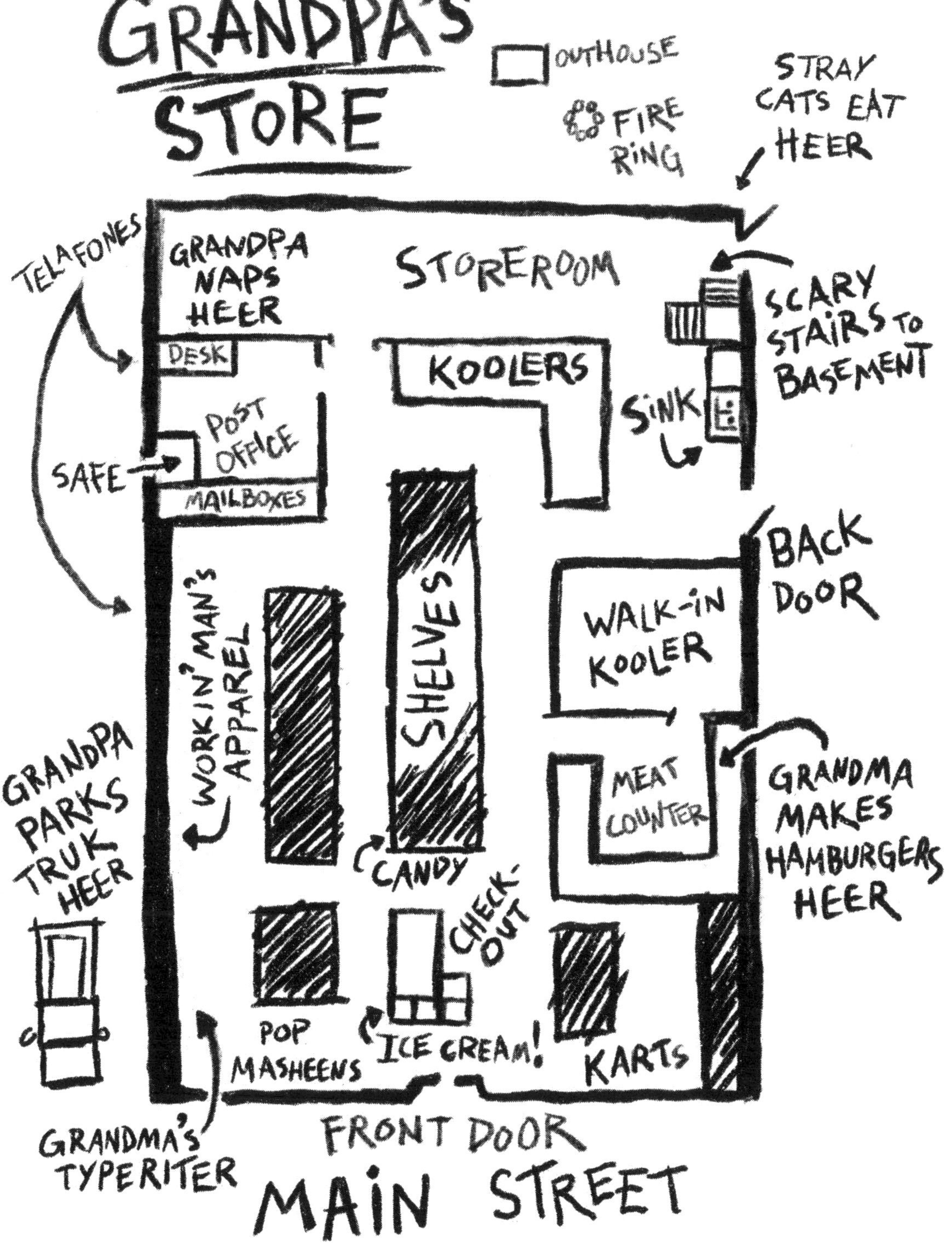
GRANDPA'S STORE
OUTHOUSE
FIRE RING
STRAY CATS EAT HEER
TELAFONES
GRANDPA NAPS HEER
STOREROOM
SCARY STAIRS TO BASEMENT
DESK
KOOLERS
SINK
POST OFFICE
SAFE
MAILBOXES
BACK DOOR
WORKIN' MAN'S APPAREL
SHELVES
WALK-IN KOOLER
GRANDPA PARKS TRUK HEER
MEAT COUNTER
GRANDMA MAKES HAMBURGERS HEER
CANDY
CHECK-OUT
POP MASHEENS
ICE CREAM!
KARTS
GRANDMA'S TYPERITER
FRONT DOOR
MAIN STREET

TROUBLE IN THE POST OFFICE

Little Frank was swatting at flies when the back door of the country store slammed shut.

"Hello, Dillard," yelled the familiar voice of the mail carrier.

The daily mail had arrived at the post office and Little Frank ran to the back of the store to see what had been delivered—a large canvas mailbag sat on the floor beside his Grandpa Dillard.

"Grandpa," asked Little Frank, "who is going to put the mail into the mailboxes this morning?"

Grandpa sat at his desk and looked over the top of his glasses. "Well, that depends," he said. "I need a good worker who's honest and cheap."

"Me, me, I am!" said Little Frank.

"All right," chuckled Grandpa. "You can help."

Ten minutes later, Little Frank was helping fill mailboxes so the locals could pick up their mail. Grandpa would pull an item from the mailbag and say, "Frank, put this letter into Box 701," or "Fold this magazine and slide it into that mailbox there."

All the while, Little Frank noticed that some people were getting more mail than others. He wondered why Grandpa's friend, Mr. Halt, received an airplane magazine and two letters, while other mailboxes remained empty. There was also Ms. Birdie, who received a small package and several envelopes with the letters B-I-L-L printed in red across their fronts. Little Frank didn't think that she should get all of the letters from a man named Bill.

As they finished, Little Frank asked, "Grandpa, why do some people get more mail than others? It isn't fair."

Grandpa had begun looking for his keys and replied, "Just the way it is, young man. I've got to take this letter up the road and will be back in a half-hour. Hop down from there and run up to Grandma."

Grandpa walked away and Little Frank began to crawl down from the mailboxes, but hesitated. He thought about how happy everyone would be to get at least one piece of mail. He also thought about how he'd like to have a look at Mr. Halt's magazine. After all, he loved airplanes and hadn't received anything either.

Little Frank made sure he was alone, because he was never to touch the mail without Grandpa or Grandma. Then he reached up, slowly at first, and then quickly began moving mail from the full mailboxes to the less full or empty mailboxes. Little Frank continued this way until the mail was distributed much more fairly by his estimate. He even found flyers advertising a local car dealership. His father had asked him to throw these flyers away many times, and Little Frank thought he'd save folks the trouble, so he tossed them into the trashcan along with the plastic wrapper from Mr. Halt's magazine. Then he crawled down from the mailboxes and rushed off thinking about the lunch he could smell cooking on Grandma's griddle.

Little Frank was eating lunch at the checkout counter when he heard the front door of the store open. Mr. Halt walked in, gave a friendly nod, and made his way back to the post office. Little Frank could hear a mailbox door squeak open and then close with a click. Mr. Halt returned to the front of the store carrying his mail, or at least part of it. He left with a friendly "Goodbye!" and hadn't noticed the airplane magazine open on the counter. That was a relief to Little Frank who had hoped to get it back in the mailbox before Mr. Halt's arrival. But he would return it, and had made up his mind to say nothing about his handiwork in the post office. So far, no one had noticed a thing.

A steady stream of regulars came and went from the store early that afternoon and some picked up their mail.

One woman said, "Mr. Dillard, there's a letter in my box that isn't mine."

"All right, thank you," replied Grandpa, not concerned.

Soon after, Ms. Birdie stopped by and asked about a package she was expecting. Grandpa thought he'd remembered the package, but it wasn't in her mailbox and he told her he'd phone if it came with the late drop-off. By the time a man handed Grandpa one of Ms. Birdie's envelopes from Bill, he knew something had happened.

Grandpa inspected the mail and found the other misplaced items, including the magazine wrapper and discarded flyers, in the trash. It took some time, but Grandpa placed the mail in the correct mailboxes. Then he walked to one of the old coolers lining the back of the store, picked out a drink, and sat down at his desk to think.

Little Frank was passing by the post office door when Grandpa said, "Frank, come in and sit down."

Little Frank entered timidly and sat on the short wooden stool beside the desk. He glanced at the mailboxes on the wall, wondering if Grandpa knew he had touched the mail without asking.

"Young man," Grandpa said, "something has happened that you and I need to investigate."

Little Frank knew what had happened, and also knew enough to act surprised and curious.

Grandpa continued, "Somebody has tampered with the mail, which is a serious crime according to the United States government. As postmaster, I'll have to report this crime to the police. I'm going to need your help with the investigation, and we'll get Sheriff Bow-Wow involved right away."

Little Frank was worried. He'd moved the mail and even borrowed some, but he'd meant no

harm. Now the police were going to be involved and he might be in real trouble. But he had been silent for too long and Grandpa was waiting for a response. All Little Frank thought to say was, "Who is Sheriff Bow-Wow?"

"Ah," said Grandpa, "when Sheriff Bow-Wow was a young detective, he was given this name because he could track criminals like a bloodhound. He always caught them, no matter what. Now he investigates mail crimes like the one that occurred in this post office today."

Little Frank was sorry he'd asked. It wouldn't take long for Grandpa and Sheriff Bow-Wow to figure out who had tampered with the mail. He wished his little sister had been around as an accomplice to share the blame—most of the blame if he told his version of the events. But she wasn't there and he'd need to tell the truth, just not yet.

"Grandpa," Little Frank asked, "can you and I investigate and skip calling the sheriff?"

"No," said Grandpa. "We've got a phone call to make."

Grandpa kept an old telephone at the corner of his desk. He picked up the handset and held it to his ear while dialing a number. After a few seconds he said, "Hello, I'd like to speak with Sheriff Bow-Wow."

Little Frank couldn't hear the voice on the other end of the phone, but he looked intently at Grandpa and hung on every word.

"Sheriff, this is Mr. Dillard down here at the post office."

Apparently the two had spoken before.

"Doing fine, thank you," said Grandpa into the handset.

Little Frank imagined the sheriff had a big nose and ears, wore a freshly ironed police uniform, and spoke deep and slow.

Grandpa continued, "I'm calling about a very serious matter today. Yes sir, someone has tampered with the mail—they've even taken a man's magazine."

Little Frank's heart was racing because Grandpa and the sheriff knew about the magazine, and it was time to come clean. Feeling mostly sorry he'd been caught, Little Frank

said, "I did it, Grandpa. I know I wasn't supposed to touch the mail, but some people didn't have any."

Grandpa cupped the handset with his hand, listening to Little Frank. "What about those items in the trash?" Grandpa asked.

"I was going to return the magazine and nobody reads those old flyers," said Little Frank.

"Sheriff, turns out I've got the suspect here, but can we discuss the charges before you come up?" asked Grandpa.

Mr. Dillard glanced at Little Frank and reached his free hand over to the shoulder of the visibly shaken boy.

"My, that's serious, sheriff," continued Grandpa. "He is just a boy after all. I don't know if he can afford to pay $1,000."

Little Frank wasn't sure how much that was, but knew it was more than the six dollars in his piggy bank at home. That worry passed when Grandpa said, "How long do you want him in jail, sheriff?"

There are moments in a child's life that he will never forget, and for Little Frank, this was one of them. He never thought he might go to jail. Being away from his family and locked up with a bunch of robbers seemed awful scary. Tears began to stream down his face.

"Well, sheriff," Grandpa continued, "it seems we ought to consider our options before we lock a young man up."

For the first time, Little Frank thought his grandpa might help him with this mess.

Mr. Dillard continued, "Now I agree that tampering with the mail is a serious offense. Mail is important to people and it needs to get to where it's going. Folks receive official documents, letters from loved ones, maybe even their favorite magazines. As postmaster, it's my job to make sure people receive that mail. They trust me."

Grandpa was talking to Sheriff Bow-Wow, but Little Frank felt like he was talking straight to him. He'd begun to understand that what he'd done was wrong.

Grandpa continued, "I know I'm asking a lot, sheriff, but would you consider letting me handle things from here? I think he's learned his lesson."

Grandpa listened to the sheriff and then asked Little Frank, "Have you got Mr. Halt's magazine?"

Little Frank nodded and pulled the rolled up magazine from his back pocket.

"Sheriff, it's here, and rest assured this won't happen again," said Grandpa, before a final pause and "Goodbye."

Grandpa hung up the phone and turned to Little Frank. "You're fortunate Sheriff Bow-Wow didn't arrest you today, and we need to agree on two things."

Little Frank was happy to agree with anything that didn't involve the sheriff.

"First, you must never tamper with the mail again. Is that understood?" asked Grandpa.

Little Frank nodded.

"Second," continued Grandpa, "we'll return Mr. Halt's magazine with an apology note. I'll draft the note, and you'll sign it."

"All right, Grandpa," agreed Little Frank.

Grandpa wrote the apology in his fine cursive penmanship, and Little Frank signed his name in big messy letters. Then they put the note and airplane magazine into the mailbox for Mr. Halt, who picked them up the following afternoon.

"I was a boy once," Mr. Halt told Grandpa on his way out of the store. "And tell Frank he can have my airplane magazines when I'm through reading them."

A short time later, Little Frank was helping in the post office when Grandpa received a call. "Post office, Dillard speaking," answered Grandpa into the telephone. "Why hello, Sheriff Bow-Wow."

Little Frank wondered what the sheriff wanted but couldn't make out what was being discussed. He soon heard Grandpa say, "I know he's capable, but I'll ask if he's willing."

Grandpa turned towards Little Frank and said, "Sheriff Bow-Wow would like to make you deputy sheriff of this post office. Are you up to the task?"

"Yes!" Little Frank replied.

"It's a big job," stressed Grandpa.

"I can do it," said Little Frank, confidently.

"You have a new deputy," said Grandpa to Sheriff Bow-Wow, "and he'll make you proud."

Grandpa hung up the phone that day knowing he wouldn't need to call Sheriff Bow-Wow again. He had a trustworthy helper in Little Frank, and a deputy sheriff who could handle any trouble in the post office. Grandma even suggested that Little Frank send folks a letter if they hadn't received one. He liked that idea, and sometimes the locals would open their mailboxes and find a solitary note from Little Frank—tucked inside a sealed envelope and stamped, of course.

THE END

THE LITTLE FIREMAN

There was a fire ring behind the country store where Grandpa told stories to his grandchildren. The fire ring was surrounded by tall grass and sat near an old wooden outhouse, which was the only bathroom for the store.

One autumn afternoon, Grandpa said, "Frank, we're going to have a bonfire at quitin' time."

Little Frank was excited and began preparations. He gathered twigs and dry leaves and put them into the fire ring. He also filled a bucket with water and set it in his wagon nearby. As he pulled the wagon to the fire ring, he mimicked all of the noises a fire truck would make. He stopped with "choosh" and sat down to wait for Grandpa, who would soon join him with a package of marshmallows and an embellished story about some Wild West adventure.

After a short time, Little Frank heard footsteps behind him. He turned his head and saw Leon Purdy walking toward the outhouse.

Leon was a heavyset man who sauntered through life. He lived nearby with his wife and five young children, including a set of twins. Leon would frequent the outhouse when temperatures were pleasant. This puzzled Little Frank because he had an indoor bathroom of his own. But the Purdys were an unruly bunch, and this was one of the few places where Leon could get a moment of quiet.

As Leon opened the outhouse door and stepped inside, he said, "How you doing, Frank?"

"I'm fine, Mr. Purdy," he replied.

Then the door swung shut, allowing Leon to finish his crossword puzzle and take a short nap.

No sooner had Leon disappeared than Little Frank heard a dog yelp and run around the corner of the store. When he craned his neck to see what had caused the commotion, Eddie Burns came into sight, wearing his high top sneakers, tattered jeans and an oversized jacket. Eddie was older and Little Frank feared him because he was a bully.

"If it ain't Fireman Frank," said Eddie, as he neared the fire ring.

It was too late to run and Little Frank's eyes avoided Eddie's gaze.

"Looks like you're ready for a fire," said Eddie in a mean kind of way. "I heard you pretending to be a fireman."

"I'm ready," said Little Frank, "but I'm waiting for my grandpa because I can't start fires on my own."

"Little boys can't start fires, but men can," said Eddie, with a puffed out chest. "I'm going up yonder to smoke a cigarette and got a couple of matches in my pocket. I'll spare one for our fire."

"No," said Little Frank, wondering when it had become *their* fire. "I've got to wait for Grandpa."

Little Frank glanced toward the outhouse hoping Mr. Purdy would come to his rescue, but the only thing coming from the outhouse was the faint sound of snoring.

"Oh, come on," said Eddie, pulling a match from his pocket. He struck the match against one of the stones lining the fire ring and tossed it into the center. The tinder caught fire right away, and Eddie saw an opportunity to further rile Little Frank. "Why don't you show me your firefighting skills, Fireman Frank," he teased.

Eddie picked up one of the long forks used to roast marshmallows, stabbed it into the burning leaves, and pulled some from the fire. He held them near the dense dry grass that surrounded the fire ring and yelled, "I need a fireman so this grass don't catch fire!"

Little Frank was uncomfortable, yet amused by this game. He pulled his wagon to the burning leaves and dumped some water from the bucket inside, quenching the fire. Eddie wasted no time pulling another fork full of leaves from the fire, and Little Frank followed with his wagon and bucket. They repeated this several times, and each time, Eddie grew more careless with his makeshift torch.

Suddenly, burning leaves flew from Eddie's fork into the grass and the fire began to grow. Both boys froze for a moment, wondering what to do.

"Gimme that bucket," yelled Eddie.

He grabbed the bucket and dumped what little water was left onto the rising flames, but it did little to quench them.

"Shoot," he said, "I'm outta here," and ran off, leaving Little Frank alone.

The fire moved quickly and surrounded the outhouse. Little Frank had to do something because Leon Purdy was asleep inside and it wouldn't take long for the flames to consume the wood around him.

"Mr. Purdy, there's a fire!" yelled Little Frank, as he grabbed a rock and threw it hard against the wall of the outhouse. The thud of the rock, along with Little Frank's shouting, startled Leon awake, and a great deal of commotion came from inside.

He emerged a moment later, bewildered and holding up his britches. "What in tarnation?" shouted Leon.

Leon hadn't run in years, and the added trouble with his pants caused him to fall several times as he escaped the flames. Little Frank watched the spectacle and thought it likely that Mr. Purdy's outhouse days were over.

With Leon shaken but safe, Little Frank realized the flames were moving quickly towards the store. The grass grew against the wooden walls of the storeroom at the back of the building, and they were ripe for a fire. Little Frank thought about telling Grandpa, but the firehouse was nearby and there was little time. He set off running as fast as he could in that direction, knowing he would have to get there quickly if the store was to be saved.

After a minute, he arrived and found Uncle Jimmy inside the big door where the fire truck was parked. His uncle was a fireman and always enjoyed visits from Little Frank.

"Well good afternoon, Frank," said his uncle.

Little Frank was out of breath and just managed to point in the direction of the store and yell, "Fire!"

Smoke was visible and his uncle sprang into action, first sounding the firehouse siren and then climbing into his fire gear. Little Frank hoped the firemen would make it in time.

The fire truck pulled out of the station and drove up the road toward the store with its sirens wailing, "wee woo, wee woo." It downshifted and pulled into the yard just as the fire began to crawl up the back wall of the store. Mr. Dillard and Leon Purdy were outside with a short garden hose, but were losing the battle. Uncle Jimmy and the other firemen climbed out of the pump truck, stretched the fire hose, and began to spray the flames with water.

Minutes later, the fire was out, but the back of the country store was damaged and there was no longer an outhouse. Smoke hung thick in the air and a dozen onlookers gathered around. The town sheriff was last to arrive.

Little Frank joined his grandpa, Uncle Jimmy and the sheriff as they surveyed the damage.

Grandpa asked, "How'd the fire start?"

His uncle pointed to the fire ring and then everyone looked at Little Frank. Little Frank hadn't considered that people might think he'd started the fire. But who else could have done it? He was preparing for a bonfire and nobody had seen Eddie.

Before Little Frank spoke up, a voice from behind them said, "I seen it all, Mr. Dillard. I can tell you what happened."

They turned around and there stood Eddie Burns.

Eddie had returned to the country store out of curiosity, but had stayed because he was afraid Little Frank would tell on him.

He continued, "I was sittin' up behind the store trying to rescue a kitten stuck in a tree when I looked over and seen Little Frank strikin' matches. Being the only man nearby, I reckoned I should stop him, but he lit that grass on fire before I could get there."

Eddie was lying through his teeth and Little Frank was worried he'd catch all of the blame. He was about to speak again but was interrupted, this time by Darcy Williams, who was eavesdropping nearby.

Darcy lived near the Purdys and could see the fire ring from her kitchen window. Darcy had plenty of time to keep an eye on her neighbors and knew all of the local gossip. This was often an irritation to folks, but this time Little Frank was relieved that someone may have seen Eddie.

"You should be ashamed of yourself, young man," said Darcy to Eddie, wagging her skinny finger in his direction. "That boy was minding his own business when you walked up and began hassling him."

Eddie looked at his shoes not bothering with a defense.

"You lit that grass on fire and then you ran off. Little Frank saved Leon and the store."

"Did you phone this in, Darcy?" asked the sheriff.

"Of course," she said. "I called several of my friends."

"How about the firehouse, Darcy? Did you call them?"

"I was getting around to it and knew Frank had things under control," she said.

The sheriff looked at her in disbelief. But Darcy was too caught up in her moment of importance to notice.

The men were not surprised that Eddie had started the fire, but they had not heard about Leon being in the outhouse. Grandpa laughed and said, "Looks like Mr. Purdy's got a story to tell."

The sheriff grinned. Then turning serious, he said, "Mr. Eddie, why don't you and I go down to the station and have a chat?"

As Eddie sulked away with the sheriff, Grandpa looked down at Little Frank. "I'm proud of you, young man," he said. "You kept a cool head in the midst of that fire. Eddie has learned a hard lesson today, and there's damage we'll need to repair, but it's nothing we can't recover from. Your quick thinking saved Mr. Purdy and the store."

His uncle agreed. He gave Little Frank a red fireman's hat and let him ride back to the station in the fire truck. As Little Frank rode in the truck, he could see his reflection in the windows of the buildings he passed by, and he did look like a real fireman!

EPILOGUE

Grandma kept the store running that afternoon, but had a little spring in her step. She had wanted an indoor bathroom at the store for years, but Grandpa had always said, "There's a perfectly good bathroom out back." Now that there wasn't a "perfectly good bathroom out back," Grandma wasted no time making plans for her new indoor bathroom. Grandpa joked that she was picking out tile as the smoke cleared, but she disputed this, saying that she was picking out tile while the flames were still hot.

THE END

HIGH WATER RESCUE

Rain pounded the roof of the country store and weather alerts sounded from the small radio at the checkout counter. Little Frank watched a truck pass by on the road as he peered through the glass storefront. The truck moved through shallow water that covered the street—water he'd like to splash in if his Grandma would let him.

The store telephone rang at twelve-thirty and Grandma answered. "Hello, Ms. Birdie," she said. "How are you and the cats getting along?"

Little Frank listened to Grandma's conversation and imagined Ms. Birdie talking on the other end of the line. Ms. Birdie was known as "The Cat Lady" because she lived with seven cats, and probably held one of them as she spoke.

A moment later, Grandma's tone turned serious and she said, "I'll send Mr. Dillard down to have a look." Grandma hung up the phone and Little Frank followed her into the post office, where Grandpa sat with his calculator and green ledger.

"Ms. Birdie called and said the heavy rains have caused flooding at her house," said Grandma. "She asked if you'd mind going over to have a look at things."

Grandpa's forehead wrinkled as he listened. He and Grandma had owned the house for twenty years and had never seen it flood, but he agreed to check on her.

Little Frank climbed with Grandpa into his truck and they started towards Ms. Birdie's. Grandpa drove the old Ford slowly because the rain made it difficult to see out the windshield, even with the wipers working hard.

Little Frank would often walk to Ms. Birdie's carrying a hot tuna casserole and a friendly typewritten note from Grandma. Ms. Birdie didn't have any family and Grandma knew that she (and her cats) looked forward to these occasions. Today, Little Frank wondered if she and the cats would be disappointed that he didn't come with their favorite meal.

Ms. Birdie's house sat alone at the bottom of a small hill and Little Frank could see that it was surrounded by knee-deep water as they rounded the corner of her street. A creek bed ran along the edge of town not far from her house. Grandpa called it an arroyo, a Spanish word that he had picked up from years of speaking with the migrant workers who frequented the store.

"An arroyo," Grandpa explained to Little Frank, "is Spanish for stream, except these streams only fill with water during hard rains." The creek bed was flowing higher than Grandpa had ever seen it, and it had flooded the area surrounding Ms. Birdie's house.

"Look at the arrow," said Little Frank.

"Arroyo," said Grandpa, as he parked the truck on the hill above Ms. Birdie's.

Grandpa rolled his pants to above his knees, motioned for Little Frank to do the same, and together they walked towards the waterlogged house. Grandpa carried Little Frank for the last fifty yards as he waded through water, and then set him down when they reached Ms. Birdie's submerged front stoop. Grandpa knocked loudly on the front door and shouted, "Ms. Birdie, you inside?"

Little Frank and Grandpa listened intently and could just hear her say, "In here Mr. Dillard, the door is open."

Grandpa pushed the door open slowly, revealing the most peculiar sight. Ms. Birdie sat on her couch, wearing a raincoat and tall rubber boots. On her lap were a purse and a cat. In fact, all seven of the cats sat with her on the couch because the floor around them was covered by shallow water. Ms. Birdie was concerned, but much calmer than one might expect. The same could not be said for the cats, who thought themselves much too good to be in such a predicament.

"How long have you been flooded?" asked Grandpa, surprised that Ms. Birdie hadn't left or called for help earlier.

"I've had water in the house since noon," replied Ms. Birdie.

"Well, its high time you get out of here," said Grandpa. "Let's go."

"I tried to leave," said Ms. Birdie, "but the cats wouldn't go because of the water, and I'm not leaving without my cats. They're like children to me."

This was true. Ms. Birdie had trained and cared for each of her cats as if they were children, though the cats were probably more spoiled. They wore black collars embroidered with their names, and silver bells hung from each of their necks. The big cat on Ms. Birdie's lap was named Smudge and he ruled the house.

"I understand you care about these cats," said Grandpa, "but it's too dangerous to stay. They can fend for themselves."

"I told you I'm not going without them," said Ms. Birdie.

Grandpa realized that Ms. Birdie was not leaving easily. He reached for one of the cats, but it hissed and struck his hand with its claws. He pulled back quickly and knew he wouldn't be taking them out himself.

"I may have to get the fire department down here to carry you out," said Grandpa.

"Call whoever you want, but I'm not leaving without my cats," she said indignantly.

Grandpa enjoyed a good relationship with Ms. Birdie and didn't want that ruined, but this was serious.

"What do you suggest we do?" asked Grandpa.

"To be honest, I'm not sure," she said.

"You're being unreasonable."

"You're not the first to call me unreasonable, Mr. Dillard."

After a moment of silence, Little Frank asked, "What about Grandma's tuna casserole? They might follow that out of the house."

Grandpa and Ms. Birdie didn't think much of his idea at first, but warmed to it after a little thought.

"We do enjoy those casseroles," said Ms. Birdie.

Grandpa hesitated a moment and then sprang into action. He walked to the kitchen and dialed a number on her telephone. "Still works," he yelled, before speaking with someone briefly and then hanging up.

"Mrs. Dillard will have that tuna casserole ready in no time at all," said Grandpa, as he returned to the living room where Ms. Birdie, Little Frank, and the multitude of cats waited. "I'd like you to come with me and Frank to pick it up, and then we'll come back for these cats."

"I think you know I'm not leaving," said Ms. Birdie. "And as much as those cats like tuna casserole, I don't think they'll be wading through water for it."

"I don't think they'll have to," said Grandpa. "I've got an idea and we'll be back soon."

Grandpa picked up Little Frank and carried him outside to the truck. The water was still rising and they didn't have long to rescue Ms. Birdie and her cats, but Grandpa was confident they had time enough to pay a visit to Mr. Halt.

Mr. Halt owned a gas station and repair shop in town called "The Garage." He ran a good business. But he accumulated a great deal of "stuff" due to his many interests and constant tinkering. This "stuff" left his business looking like a junkyard, but like most junkyards, there were useful items that could be used in peculiar situations, and that's just what Grandpa and Little Frank needed.

Mr. Halt was standing beneath the pump canopy when they pulled up.

"Good afternoon, Dillard. Quite the rain we're having today," he said.

"A real drencher," replied Grandpa. "We've got flooding down at Ms. Birdie's and I need your help."

"Flooding?" asked Mr. Halt. "I haven't been down her way, but what is it you need?"

"Remember that flat-bottomed boat you were showing me last week?" asked Grandpa.

"Yes, my English punt," said Mr. Halt proudly. "She's built of pine and I've got her painted up real pretty now."

Little Frank was confused because he thought punt was to kick something, but he kept quiet.

"Will she fit through the front door of a house?" asked Grandpa.

"She's real skinny at the ends. You should be able to get some of her through the door," said Mr. Halt. "But why?"

"Come with us and see for yourself. I could use a hand anyway," said Grandpa.

Of course Mr. Halt agreed, and even volunteered to take the boat using his big tractor with loader forks.

"I'll meet you down by Ms. Birdie's place in a half-hour," said Grandpa.

Mr. Halt waved in agreement and went about getting his boat ready for whatever it was Mr. Dillard had planned. Meanwhile, Grandpa and Little Frank made their way back to the country store and waited for the casserole to finish cooking.

"I can't make it cook faster," said Grandma, as Grandpa paced back and forth.

When the casserole was finally ready, they piled back into the truck. Grandpa, who was seemingly confident and always thinking ahead, asked Grandma to find someone who might be willing to take in an elderly woman and seven cats for a few days.

"That should be easy," quipped Grandma.

Minutes later, Grandpa and Mr. Halt were wading through the water on either side of the flat-bottomed boat, and Little Frank sat inside with the casserole. It had been nearly an hour since they had left, and though the rain had stopped, the water had risen several inches. As they reached the house, Little Frank hoped Ms. Birdie was safe, but was mostly worried about holding the bait for seven agitated and hungry cats.

Ms. Birdie and her feline companions hadn't moved since Grandpa and Little Frank last saw them, but the water in the house now covered much of her boots.

"I was about to get my snorkel," she joked, as Grandpa stuck his head through the doorway.

"You would have needed eight," replied Grandpa, as he pulled part of the boat through the doorway with Mr. Halt's help. "We're getting you out now before the water rises any higher."

The cats caught the scent of their favorite meal and stirred excitedly while Little Frank sat anticipating the onslaught.

Grandpa helped a smiling Ms. Birdie into the boat, the front of which was only a few feet from the couch. Smudge was the first cat to jump aboard, and the others followed in no certain order, with two or three leaping at a time.

Just as he had feared, the cats crowded around Little Frank hoping to get their share of the casserole. Then something unexpected happened: Smudge jumped up and sat right beside Little Frank. He began to swat and hiss at the other cats, seemingly disgusted at their lack of manners. The cats grew calm and Smudge sat proudly as if he were the hero and captain of the ship, leading his feline companions from danger.

Grandpa and Mr. Halt steadily pushed the boat to the edge of the water, where they helped Ms. Birdie onto dry ground. Little Frank climbed out of the boat next, followed by Smudge and the other cats. The cats still looked eagerly at the casserole Little Frank held in his hands, but they remained calm under Smudge's command. This amused Grandpa and he asked Ms. Birdie and Little Frank if they were willing to lead the cats to the country store on foot.

"I think they'll follow," said Grandpa.

Everyone agreed, so Little Frank and Ms. Birdie began their walk, followed by Smudge and the other cats, all lined up in a row. "That's the darndest thing," chuckled Mr. Halt.

As the motley bunch rounded the corner and began to walk up Main Street, the locals took notice, and stepped outside to admire the grand procession. Normally the dogs in town would have given chase to the cats, but they were too perplexed by what they saw. Little Frank and Ms. Birdie marched the cats right up to the country store where Grandma met them with a smile.

"I'm glad everyone's safe," she said. "Ms. Birdie, why don't we let the cats enjoy their casserole while you and I go inside and arrange a place for you to stay?"

"That sounds wonderful," said Ms. Birdie, feeling grateful for the Dillards' help.

Grandpa unfolded his newspaper the next morning and read the headline, "Rainstorm Pummels Region." The storm and consequent flooding had made front-page news, and there below the headline, in the middle of the page, was a picture of Ms. Birdie, Little Frank, and the cats marching up Main Street.

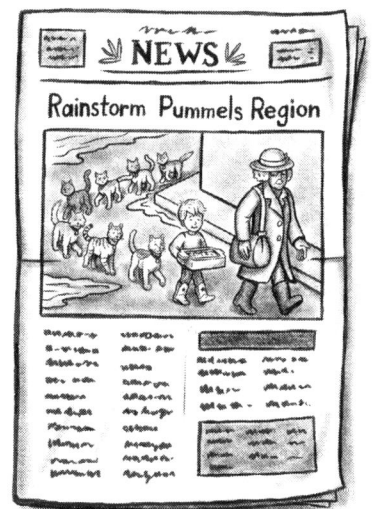

Grandpa smiled as he handed the newspaper to Grandma. "Imagine how excited Frank will be to have his picture in the newspaper," he said.

"He'll be very excited," agreed Grandma. "And it's a good thing this picture was taken."

"Why is that?" asked Grandpa.

"Because Frank is going to tell this story to everyone he meets, and he'll need a picture as proof if anyone's going to believe him. After all, a story about a boy and his Grandpa rescuing an old woman and her cats with a tuna casserole, and then marching them up Main Street, is pretty far-fetched."

THE END

GRANDMA'S HAMBURGERS

Little Frank was enjoying a hamburger Grandma had made for him when Leon Purdy walked into the country store.

"Frank, that burger sure smells good," Mr. Purdy said. "Why don't I give you a dollar bill for half of it?"

Little Frank liked his hamburger and didn't think that sounded like a good trade, so he declined, but Mr. Purdy had children of his own and knew how to bargain.

He held up two coins, admired them, and then said, "I'll give you the dollar, plus these two shiny quarters."

Little Frank liked the quarters, so the exchange was made, and Mr. Purdy ate his half of the hamburger before Little Frank could get the coins and wadded up bill into his pocket.

"That sure is a good burger. Worth every penny," said Leon.

When Leon spotted Grandma behind the meat counter he continued, "Mrs. Dillard, let me know when you start selling those burgers. Me and the Mrs. will be your best customers."

Grandma didn't doubt this would be true but politely reminded him that she wasn't interested in running a restaurant.

"Well, you ought to consider it," he said, before walking back for a gallon of milk.

Grandma didn't know it at the time, but just one week later she would agree to sell her hamburgers. The person who would convince her to do this was the Dillards' good friend, Pastor Green.

Pastor Green was chatting with Grandpa in the post office that following Saturday when Grandma stepped in to say hello.

"Good to see you, Mrs. Dillard. I've been thinking about you," he said.

"This sounds like trouble," said Grandpa, grinning at Grandma.

Pastor Green chuckled and said, "Maybe so, Dillard. As you know, the church youth are going on a mission trip to Tennessee this summer."

Grandpa nodded and said, "Near Nashville, right?"

"Yes, that's right. We're going to host a meal and talent show to raise money for the trip," said Pastor Green. "I don't know if we've got much talent," he added with a wink, "but what we can give folks is a special meal, and I think Mrs. Dillard's hamburgers are very special indeed."

Pastor Green was right about Grandma's hamburgers, just as Leon and many others had been. The hamburgers were, as Grandpa put it, "delectable." Nobody knew what made them so good. Perhaps it was Grandma's old griddle, her buttered white bread, or Grandpa's freshly ground beef. Maybe it was the combination of all those things. Grandma didn't cook them for many folks either, making them all the more sought-after.

Both Grandpa and Pastor Green looked at Grandma, who stood silently with her arms crossed.

"I'd like to help, but I'm not set up to make hamburgers for a large crowd. Plus, I'm not

sure my hamburgers are suitable for such an event," Grandma said. "Maybe I can organize a potluck."

"I know you don't want to go into the restaurant business, but your hamburgers will draw a crowd because they are delicious," said Pastor Green. "This will be a one-time deal, and a wonderful opportunity for you to help the youth and the people of Tennessee."

She replied, "Thank you for the kind words, pastor, but…"

"But I don't need an answer right away," interrupted Pastor Green, "You can let me know in a few days."

Grandma smiled at the pastor's persistence and agreed to think things over, but Grandma loved helping people and Pastor Green left the store knowing what her answer would be. She just needed a little time.

When Pastor Green returned, Grandma did agree to cook for the fundraiser, and was even excited about it. She and Grandpa sat with the pastor that afternoon and worked out the necessary administrative details. It was decided that the event would be held at the community church and would be called, "On Mission for Volunteers."

Signs for the fundraiser were hung at nearly every street corner in town, but they probably weren't necessary. Word about Grandma's hamburgers had spread quickly and most locals were already planning to attend.

Little Frank was asking about the fundraiser one afternoon when Grandpa suggested, "Why don't you and I perform in the talent show?"

"Perform what?" asked Little Frank.

"Well," replied Grandpa, "you and I can carry a tune, and I can play the piano a little. I think we ought to sing, 'Gotta Quit Kickin' My Dog Around.'"

"Oh yes," said Little Frank. "That's one of my favorite songs!"

Grandpa had learned the song as a child and could play it by ear on the piano. He played it often for Little Frank, who found the lyrics rather peculiar and pestered Grandpa with questions each time it was sung.

"Grandpa, who's the dog, and why are they kicking him around?" Little Frank would ask.

"It's just a silly old song," Grandpa would reply. "It's about a hound dog that goes to town and gets harassed by some troublemakers."

"Poor old hound," Little Frank would say. "Is he all right?"

"Yes, he's fine," Grandpa would reply each time.

"Ok, let's sing it again!" Little Frank would say. And they always did.

The evening of the fundraiser finally arrived and there was a buzz in the air. Grandma and some close friends were in the kitchen making last minute preparations. The sanctuary was decorated, the pews had been replaced with tables, and a big banner over the stage read, "On Mission for Volunteers. Join Us in Helping People in the Volunteer State."

An admission ticket bought one hamburger, plus sides and entertainment from performers in the talent show. A line ran around the block and was filled with people eager to hand their money over. Leon Purdy and his family were at the front of the line, and he purchased three extra tickets to make sure he got his fill of Grandma's hamburgers.

"There's about to be a lawsuit," he said to his wife as he waited impatiently. "My stomach is suing my throat for lack of support."

Mrs. Purdy rolled her eyes and patted Leon's big belly while saying, "I'm confident you're not going to starve."

Eddie Burns also stood in line, looking uncomfortable because he hadn't been to church in a while, but was unwilling to miss out on the excitement.

Grandma and her friends began serving hamburgers as soon as the doors opened. She cooked every beef patty on her griddle, and her friends assembled the hamburgers exactly as she had instructed. Much to Grandma's surprise, the meal did not disappoint.

"This is the best burger west of the Mississippi," one man said.

"How does she do it?" a woman asked nearby.

Of course Leon was pleased as punch and had eaten four hamburgers before the night was over. He even tried to talk his children out of their food, but had little success.

As folks finished eating, Pastor Green stood and welcomed everyone to the event. He thanked Grandma for the fine cooking and told about how grateful the youth and the people of Tennessee would be for the money raised. He didn't miss the opportunity to speak to the un-churched in the crowd, either. He gave a short but rousing sermon about serving others and living a God-honoring life. Many in the crowd were moved, including Eddie, who secretly promised to quit his bullying.

With everyone full of food and in good spirits following the pastor's remarks, the talent show began.

Ms. Birdie and her cat, Smudge, were the first act of the night. Ms. Birdie sat proudly on stage with a plastic hoop that Smudge jumped through on command. After each jump, he would stand on his hind legs and wave his paws at his adoring fans. At the end he received a treat and bowed with Ms. Birdie in front of the cheering crowd.

Next came a boy named Timmy Johnson, an up-and-coming calf-roper who was skilled with a lasso. He was dressed like a cowboy, but horses and calves weren't allowed in the church, so he stood and lassoed a number of stationary objects and his dog, Buck. Buck wasn't enthused about the arrangement, but was well-trained and wound up being a real crowd pleaser.

Several acts followed including a pair of jugglers, an old man with some nifty card tricks, plus Rosie and Bernice Johnson—two sisters who impressed folks with their line dancing.

Grandpa and Little Frank followed the dancing girls and were last to perform. They wore coonskin caps and called themselves the Hillbilly Duet. Grandpa played the piano and they sang:

> *As we went by the country store*
> *A bunch of boys came out the door…*
> *They tied a tin can to old Tim's tail*
> *And ran him past the county jail…*
> *Every time I go to town*
> *The boys keep kickin' my dog around*
> *Makes no difference if he is a hound*
> *They gotta quit kickin' my dog around*

It wasn't a beautiful rendition, but it was fun and the crowd clapped and sang along for the final chorus. Grandpa stood at the end and joked that the Hillbilly Duet would be touring, but only in towns where they were famous, so they weren't expecting to be on the road for long. Little Frank was relieved to hear they'd be returning soon because he hadn't packed or let his mom know he would be going away.

Pastor Green spoke at the end of the evening and thanked everyone for attending. He also announced that Timmy Johnson had won the talent show based on his lasso skills and his well-trained companion. Timmy took home a small trophy, a Bible, and some dog bones for Buck's enjoyment. The fundraiser had been a great success and the townspeople left feeling glad to have helped the youth and the needy in Tennessee.

Little Frank saw Grandma in church the following morning and said, "Grandma, everyone really liked your hamburgers. Can we sell them in front of the store sometime?"

Grandma smiled at Little Frank and said, "I'm not interested in running a hamburger stand. Plus, I'm not set up to make hamburgers for a large crowd."

"It sure would be fun," said Little Frank. "And everyone would come."

Grandma smiled and replied, "I appreciate your persistence, but…"

"But you can think about it," interrupted Little Frank. And he ran off knowing what her answer would be. She just needed a little time.

THE END

A THIEF IN THE NIGHT

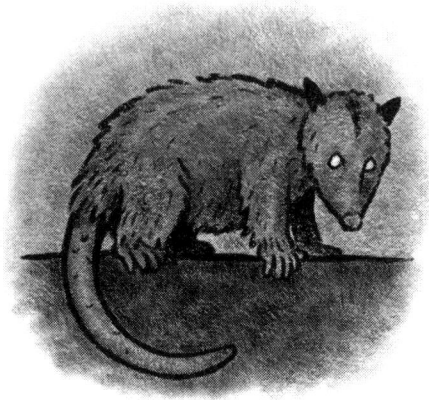

"Frank, come have a look at this," said Grandpa from the back of the country store.

Grandpa fidgeted with the toothpick between his lips as he looked at the dog food strewn across the floor. Something was living in the storeroom and enjoying nighttime meals at Grandpa's expense. It had feasted on bananas the night before.

"Is it a thief?" asked Little Frank.

"Of sorts," replied Grandpa. "I don't think it's a person, though. Probably an animal, seeing how this bag is torn."

"I think it's a mouse," said Little Frank. Then he paused and said, "or a bear!"

"No, it's bigger than a mouse but smaller than a bear," said Grandpa. "You and I need to find out what we're dealing with, though. I can't keep feeding whatever is loose in here."

"How do we find it?" asked Little Frank, excited that he'd been enlisted to help.

"By catching it in the act of thievery," replied Grandpa. "And I'm guessing this thief is nocturnal, so we'll need to stay up late if we want to catch it."

"You think it's in the army, Grandpa?"

"What do you mean, young man?"

"You said it's a colonel." Little Frank had heard Grandpa mention this word when talking about his time in the army.

Grandpa laughed and replied, "I said nocturnal and it means the animal we're dealing with is asleep days and awake nights."

Little Frank thought that sounded strange, but then he remembered Ms. Birdie's cats sometimes slept during the day. Maybe it was one of them.

After the store closed that evening, Grandpa and Little Frank sat in the post office and ate the supper Grandma had made for them. Little Frank paused between each bite to listen for movement in the storeroom.

"Relax, Frank," Grandpa kept saying. "It won't be out for a bit, especially with us making noise."

Little Frank wasn't so sure. He quickly finished his food so they could get to the business of waiting for the thief. Grandpa finished most of his meal but left the last few bites to use as bait for the animal.

Little Frank and Grandpa made their way to a sleeping bag and pillows that lay between neatly stacked boxes in the storeroom. Grandpa sometimes took afternoon naps and he would come here to lie down. They turned out the lights and Little Frank settled in close to Grandpa, partly because the space was cramped, but also because he was scared of what may be lurking in the dark.

"Grandpa," said Little Frank. "Have you had a thief in the store before?"

"Several," said Grandpa, "but none more memorable than a man named Shorty and his wife, LuAnn. Shorty was a soft-spoken man with a stature fitting his name. LuAnn was as loud as she was large, and would wear an oversized coat into the store. Shorty would make small talk with your Grandma at the front counter while LuAnn wandered the aisles stuffing

her coat with food and other items. Then she'd make her way to the front and purchase something inexpensive like gum. You see what they were doing, don't you?"

"Stealing!" said Little Frank.

"Yes," said Grandpa. "They worked as a team and stole what she had stuffed in her coat."

"Did you catch them?"

"It didn't take long for us to figure out what they were up to," said Grandpa. "I set a coat rack by the front door and we asked LuAnn to hang her coat there when she visited. They stopped shopping with us soon after; moved onto other places, I guess."

Grandpa and Little Frank sat clutching their flashlights, eager to confront the intruder. It would undoubtedly like a taste of Grandpa's dinner that lay on the plate near the foot of his sleeping bag. But it wasn't long before Grandpa and Little Frank were asleep, both unaware that something was creeping towards them from across the room.

CRASH! Grandpa and Little Frank were jolted awake. Grandpa quickly switched on the flashlight and shone it straight ahead. Something had turned the plate over, but what? Grandpa moved the light to the right and then to the left, but saw nothing. Then Grandpa and Little Frank saw them at the same time: two eyes were glowing in the dark just above the light. Grandpa pointed the flashlight up and revealed the thief. A motionless creature sat on a shelf across the room. It looked like a giant mouse, but had black and white fur, a long snout, and an even longer tail.

"What is it?" whispered Little Frank.

"Why, it's an opossum," said Grandpa. "Follow me."

He calmly stood up and walked out of the storeroom with Little Frank in tow. The opossum and Little Frank watched each other closely, mostly out of curiosity.

"Trapping that rascal may not be easy," said Grandpa, who had trapped a number of opossums before. "We'll let him hide, then we'll set the trap."

Little Frank peeked back into the storeroom a few moments later. The opossum had scurried off into the darkness, so he followed Grandpa into the basement. A large coal furnace sat near the bottom of the stairs and the rest of the area was used for storage. Little

Frank rarely visited because it seemed dark and scary. Grandpa walked to the back corner and retrieved a curious object that was several feet long, but not near as tall or wide.

"What is that?" asked Little Frank.

"It's a steel trap," replied Grandpa. "It will trap cats, raccoons…"

"Or an opossum!" Little Frank said, interrupting Grandpa.

"Yes," Grandpa replied.

"I could just catch the opossum with my fishing net," stated Little Frank.

"You think so?" asked Grandpa.

"Yes," replied Little Frank. I've caught lots of animals with my net."

"I'll tell you what," said Grandpa. "If my trap doesn't work, we'll use your fishing net."

This sounded good to Little Frank and he imagined himself catching opossums as he followed Grandpa to the front of the store, where they made their next selection.

"This is double sided-tape, so it's sticky on both sides," said Grandpa. "I'll show you what we'll do." Grandpa placed the trap on the post office desk and began to set it up. "We'll open the trap door and put food on the pan," he said. "When the opossum comes inside to eat the food, it will step on the pan and close the trap door, locking it inside. The problem is, young opossums like ours are lightweight, so they'll often steal the food in the trap without being caught. That's why we're wrapping this tape around the pan. It's just sticky enough to make the opossum trigger the door shut."

"Will it hurt?" asked Little Frank.

"Not a bit," said Grandpa, who had a soft spot for animals, even when one was stealing from him.

Next, Grandpa set a strip of fresh meat in the trap. "The opossum will love it," he said confidently. Then he and Little Frank placed the trap in the dark storeroom and closed the door. "We'll come back in the morning to see if we caught him," said Grandpa. "It's bedtime and we need to get you home."

Little Frank had only one thing on his mind when he arrived at the country store the following morning. He ran down the aisle towards the post office and yelled, "Grandpa, did we trap the opossum?"

"I haven't checked because I was waiting for you," replied Grandpa. "Let's have a look."

Little Frank followed Grandpa into the storeroom, where they found an empty trap and a missing piece of meat.

"That rascal stole another meal," said Grandpa, frustrated that he'd been outfoxed.

"I'll have to catch him with my fishing net," said Little Frank.

"Looks like we might need you to!" replied Grandpa. "How about I give you the rest of the day. We'll try the trap again if you haven't caught him by tonight."

Little Frank spent much of his morning in the storeroom opossum hunting and he kept Grandpa updated on his progress.

"It's not behind the door," he'd yell, or "I don't see it by the freezer."

Of course he had to help Grandpa with the Saturday mail, then there was lunch, plus a dozen other distractions that occupied his time. By mid-afternoon Little Frank had given up hunting, but he did sit in the storeroom with his net in case the creature decided to show itself. He passed the time finger-painting opossum pictures, and his paintings littered the floor by the time Grandpa walked in that evening.

"Have you caught the opossum?" Grandpa asked, already knowing the answer to his question.

"I think he's gone," replied Little Frank.

"I wish that were true," Grandpa said. "I think we'll give the trap another try."

This plan sounded good to Little Frank, who had grown tired of waiting for the opossum. He and Grandpa placed another strip of meat in the trap, but this time they secured it to the pan using fishing line, hoping the opossum would tug hard and trigger the trap door closed.

"That should do it," said Grandpa, though he was feeling less confident about his trapping skills. "We'll stop by tomorrow after church and see if we got it."

Grandpa opened the front door of the country store the next day and Little Frank ran ahead to the storeroom. Grandpa hadn't made it halfway back before Little Frank ran out shouting, "Grandpa, there's an orange opossum in our trap!"

"An orange opossum?" Grandpa asked, wondering what Little Frank could possibly mean. He stepped into the storeroom and sure enough, there in the trap lay the opossum, and it was orange from head to tail.

"Wow!" is all Grandpa could mutter.

"How did he get his color?" Little Frank asked.

"From your finger paints," Grandpa said.

Little Frank's finger paints lay on the floor near the trap, and the orange bottle had been left open. It was evident the finger paint had interested the opossum, leaving its fur and the surrounding floor covered in orange.

"The opossum looks like he's wearing a prison jumpsuit," said Grandpa, who was surprisingly playful given the mess in his storeroom.

"The opossum is our prisoner!" said Little Frank.

"He sure is," Grandpa said. "Now let's get him out of my store."

They cleaned up the paint and loaded the opossum into the truck, which Little Frank now imagined was a police car. They had just pulled onto the road when they spotted Mr. Halt walking. Grandpa pulled the truck alongside him and Little Frank shouted, "We've trapped a thief, and he's an opossum, and he's orange!"

"Seems you have," replied Mr. Halt, who was surprised and inquisitive. "You'd better make sure it can't get back into your store, and drop him a good distance out," he advised as Grandpa pulled away.

"My thoughts exactly," yelled Grandpa.

"Where are we going?" asked Little Frank.

"To a stand of trees that I know well," replied Grandpa. "It's a place where our thief can live without getting into trouble."

"Grandpa?" asked Little Frank. "Do you think the opossum is like Shorty?"

"What do you mean?" asked Grandpa.

"Do you think it has another opossum like LuAnn who helps it steal?"

This thought had not occurred to Grandpa and he didn't like it one bit, mainly because Little Frank could be right. There could be another opossum in the storeroom.

Grandpa looked at Little Frank and said, "Guess we had better set that trap again tonight."

"All right," said Little Frank. "Let's leave some finger paint out, too. I really like catching painted opossums!"

THE END

ROCK HUNT

Little Frank poked his head through the doorway of the post office where Grandpa and Mr. Wickerman were looking at arrowheads.

"Were your ears burnin', Frank?" asked Mr. Wickerman, turning towards the boy.

"No," said Little Frank, confident his ears felt fine.

"I told Mr. Wickerman that you were getting to be quite the rock hunter," said Grandpa, "and that we nicknamed you 'Chief Sharp Eyes'."

"I found *that* arrowhead," said Little Frank, pointing proudly to one of the rocks lying on his grandpa's desk.

"Very nice," commented Mr. Wickerman. "Dillard, "I remember when you started rock hunting. I saw you out on the dry land one afternoon staring at the ground. Do you remember what I asked?"

"Sure do," chuckled Grandpa. "You asked if I was out looking for a dime."

Mr. Wickerman grinned and said, "That's right! I didn't know what you were doing, but a dime was one of the few things you'd look that hard for."

Mr. Wickerman and Grandpa were good friends and enjoyed teasing one another. Mr. Wickerman teased Grandpa about his thriftiness and Grandpa teased Mr. Wickerman about wearing too much cologne.

"Wickerman, all these years and you've never been rock hunting with me," said Grandpa.

"There isn't much to it," said Mr. Wickerman, who knew how to get under Grandpa's skin. "You wander around, kick the dirt and pick up arrowheads."

"If you think it's that easy," replied Grandpa, "Frank and I are headed to the ranch this afternoon for a rock hunt, and we've got lunch and plenty of room for you. Perhaps you can show us how it's done."

"I suppose I have the time if lunch is included," said Mr. Wickerman, "and if I can bring Hank."

"You can bring your smelly mutt," Grandpa said.

Hank greeted everyone as they stepped out of the country store a short time later.

"Don't forget your lunch!" called Grandma from inside.

"Thank you," Grandpa replied. "See you later."

Grandpa set the lunch down in his truck and helped Little Frank, who was struggling to climb inside while holding two books and a stuffed bear.

"We're just going for a couple of hours," said Grandpa. "Do you really need all of that?"

"Yup," replied Little Frank, who carried his "special things" everywhere.

"Set your bear here in the middle, but he better not eat my lunch," Grandpa joked.

"Yum," said Little Frank, pretending to eat the food with his stuffed companion. Then he looked through the rear window of the cab to make sure Mr. Wickerman and Hank were settled into the truck bed.

Grandpa took the blacktop road out of town and into the countryside for several miles before turning down a long, unmarked, dirt road. The road led to the Dillard ranch—

land that had been handed down from Grandma's family, but was nonetheless cherished by Grandpa. The truck rolled to a stop atop a small ridge that ran across the land, and Grandpa lowered the tailgate where they would sit for lunch.

Grandpa pointed toward a stand of trees a good distance away. "There's where we dropped off that thief, the orange opossum," he said.

"I see the trees," said Little Frank. "Does the green opossum live there, too?"

"He sure does," said Grandpa, as he bit into the sandwich that Grandma had made. "This is good stuff. Do you like it?"

Both Mr. Wickerman and Little Frank nodded with full mouths.

"I've found more arrowheads on this ridge than anywhere else," said Grandpa, eager to discuss the topic.

"Why?" asked Little Frank.

"Years ago, when Moby Dick was a minnow, the Indians roamed this land hunting buffalo and they'd set up hunting camps here on this high ground."

"What did they do with the arrowheads?" asked Little Frank, like he did every time he visited the ranch.

"They'd affix rock arrowheads to wooden arrows and then shoot them with their bows," replied Grandpa. "That's how they killed buffalo. Once they had killed a buffalo, they'd march right up this hill, cook their meal, and fill their bellies."

"Good to know," stated Mr. Wickerman. "Makes me awful eager to find an arrowhead."

"Let's go," said Grandpa, finishing the last of his sandwich. "But beware of two things that bite here on the ranch: cacti and rattlesnakes. Not that you have to worry about rattlesnakes, Wickerman. The smell of your cologne should keep them away."

Mr. Wickerman pretended not to hear the comment.

Grandpa continued, "Arrowhead hunting is about knowing when and where to look. If you hunt with me, you'll generally have those things covered. And you need a keen eye, which comes with practice, so you probably won't be doing much finding, Wickerman."

The rock hunt began and Little Frank wondered if anyone would find an arrowhead. Grandpa walked slowly along the ridge carrying a shovel, though he wasn't using it to dig. Instead, he would use the tool to loosen a little dirt or push aside some grass, and occasionally scoop up a rock for closer inspection. Mr. Wickerman wandered ahead, walking quickly, and stooping frequently to grab fistfuls of rocks and sand when something caught his eye.

After a few minutes, Mr. Wickerman shouted, "Dillard, I think I've got one!" He walked to Grandpa and handed him the rock, expecting Grandpa would congratulate him on a great find.

"Yes sir," said Grandpa, studying the pointy rock with great interest. "This here is a dog rock!"

"Boy howdy!" said an excited Mr. Wickerman. "I told you I'd find an arrowhead."

"Do you know what a dog rock is good for?" asked Grandpa.

"No," replied Mr. Wickerman.

Grandpa unexpectedly tossed the rock towards Hank, who casually sniffed the ground where it landed. "That's a good rock for throwing to your dog," he said, followed by a hearty laugh.

"You mean that wasn't an arrowhead?" asked Mr. Wickerman, who was both surprised and disappointed.

"No sir," replied Grandpa. "You'll have to put in a little more work than that."

Grandpa and Mr. Wickerman continued their hunt along the ridge, but Little Frank soon fell behind. Like most boys his age, he was easily distracted, and had paused to pick some spring wildflowers. He was kneeling beside a cluster of yellow violets when he saw movement nearby. He stood up slowly while looking around, wondering what had caught his eye, and then he saw it. A rattlesnake lay coiled within striking distance, unhappy that it had been disturbed. The sound of the snake's rattle was now audible and Little Frank remembered that he shouldn't make any abrupt movements. He called for Grandpa, but his voice was lost in the prairie breeze, leaving no one to help him.

Suddenly, the snake struck. Little Frank closed his eyes. He reopened them a moment later when he didn't feel the sting of a bite, but it was difficult to see through the dusty air. Then he saw that the snake and Hank were locked in an intense battle. Hank was barking aggressively, and dancing around the snake, which was coiled and striking whenever the dog stepped too close.

Grandpa and Mr. Wickerman heard the commotion and made their way quickly to Little Frank, pulling him to safety.

"Careful, Hank!" yelled Mr. Wickerman, knowing a rattlesnake bite could kill a dog.

Hank lunged at the snake and caught him by the tail, but only briefly, as the snake struck at his face, possibly landing a bite. Hank barked again before backing away, allowing the snake to crawl under the cover of some nearby rocks.

Grandpa and Mr. Wickerman made sure Frank was unharmed, then quickly turned their attention to Hank.

"Was he bitten?" Grandpa asked.

Mr. Wickerman looked the dog over, paying careful attention to where the snake struck at his face. "There's plenty of dirt and drool," he reported, "but I don't see any signs of a bite."

Hank panted and seemed to be enjoying the attention.

"We'll keep an eye on him," said Grandpa. "He's a hero now for keeping Frank safe from that rattlesnake."

"A hero, indeed," said Mr. Wickerman, proudly patting his dog's head. Then he stood up from beside Hank, but paused. The skirmish between Hank and the rattlesnake had disturbed the ground, exposing a rock that caught Mr. Wickerman's eye. He knelt back down and used his hands to further loosen the soil around the rock, and then picked it up for a closer inspection. "Dillard," he said, "I think I've got one, a real arrowhead this time!"

"Is it another dog rock?" asked Grandpa from several feet away.

"Sort of," replied Mr. Wickerman, "Hank unearthed it."

"Let's have a look," said Grandpa, skeptically.

Grandpa took the rock and inspected it for a moment, then he paused and glanced at Mr. Wickerman before looking back at the rock.

"Well?" asked Mr. Wickerman.

"It's a nice size with high quality flaking," commented Grandpa. "The point is intact, it's beautifully notched…"

"So it's a real arrowhead?" interrupted Mr. Wickerman.

"It's a beautiful flint rock called a plains knife," said Grandpa, "one of the nicest I've ever seen."

"Wow," said Mr. Wickerman, reaching for his prized arrowhead.

"First-timer's luck found you that rock, but you and Hank deserve it for keeping Frank safe," Grandpa said. "Now let's head back to the store and close up for the evening."

Mr. Wickerman rode back to the store in the cab of the truck with Grandpa and Little Frank, while Hank dozed in back, tired from his courageous battle.

"Dillard, what's the name of that ridge we found the arrowhead on?" asked Mr. Wickerman.

"Doesn't have a name," replied Grandpa.

"What do you say we call it Rattlesnake Ridge?" suggested Mr. Wickerman.

"Rattlesnake Ridge it is," announced Grandpa.

"Rattlesnake Ridge!" seconded Little Frank in a loud voice.

Mr. Wickerman and Little Frank admired the new arrowhead as Grandpa closed up the post office that evening.

"You know, Dillard," said Mr. Wickerman. "I would normally keep this arrowhead for myself. But there's a good story behind this rock and I want you to frame it and hang it on the wall with your collection—for memory's sake."

On one wall of the post office hung arrowheads that Grandpa had found over the years, along with family photographs, newspaper cutouts, and hand drawn pictures from Little Frank depicting his adventures at the country store.

"I like your idea," said Grandpa. "We'll hang it in a frame with Little Frank's arrowhead."

"But your wall is almost full," observed Little Frank. "I don't think it will fit."

"There's a story and a fond memory behind everything on that wall," said Grandpa, "and it will never be full."

Little Frank was relieved to hear that, because he knew there would be many more memories to hang on the post office wall at Grandpa and Grandma's country store.

THE END

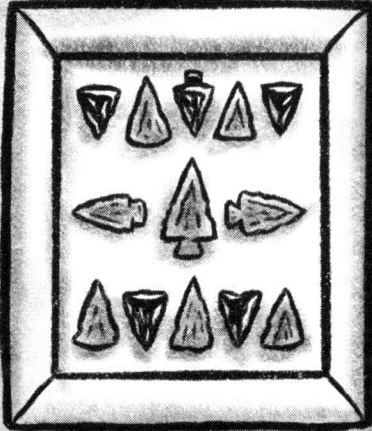